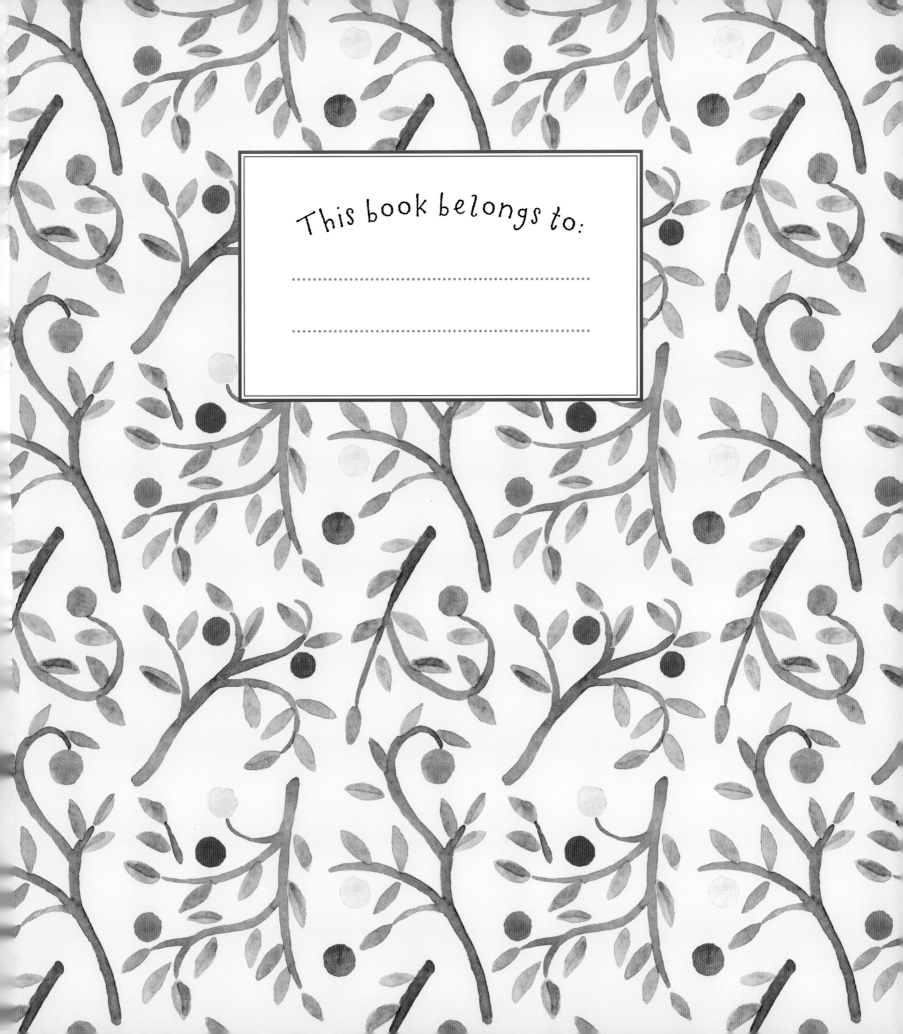

This book belongs to:

....

....

Editor: Ruth Symons
Designer: Bianca Lucas
Managing Editor: Victoria Garrard
Design Manager: Anna Lubecka

Copyright © QEB Publishing, Inc. 2013

First published in the United States by
QEB Publishing, Inc.
3 Wrigley, Suite A
Irvine, CA 92618

www.qed-publishing.co.uk

A CIP record for this book is available from the Library of Congress.

ISBN 978 1 60992 510 9

Printed in China

I'm the HAPPIEST

Anna Shuttlewood

QEB

QEB Publishing

It was a beautiful sunny day, and all
the animals were gathered together.
Giraffe had his head high in the trees.

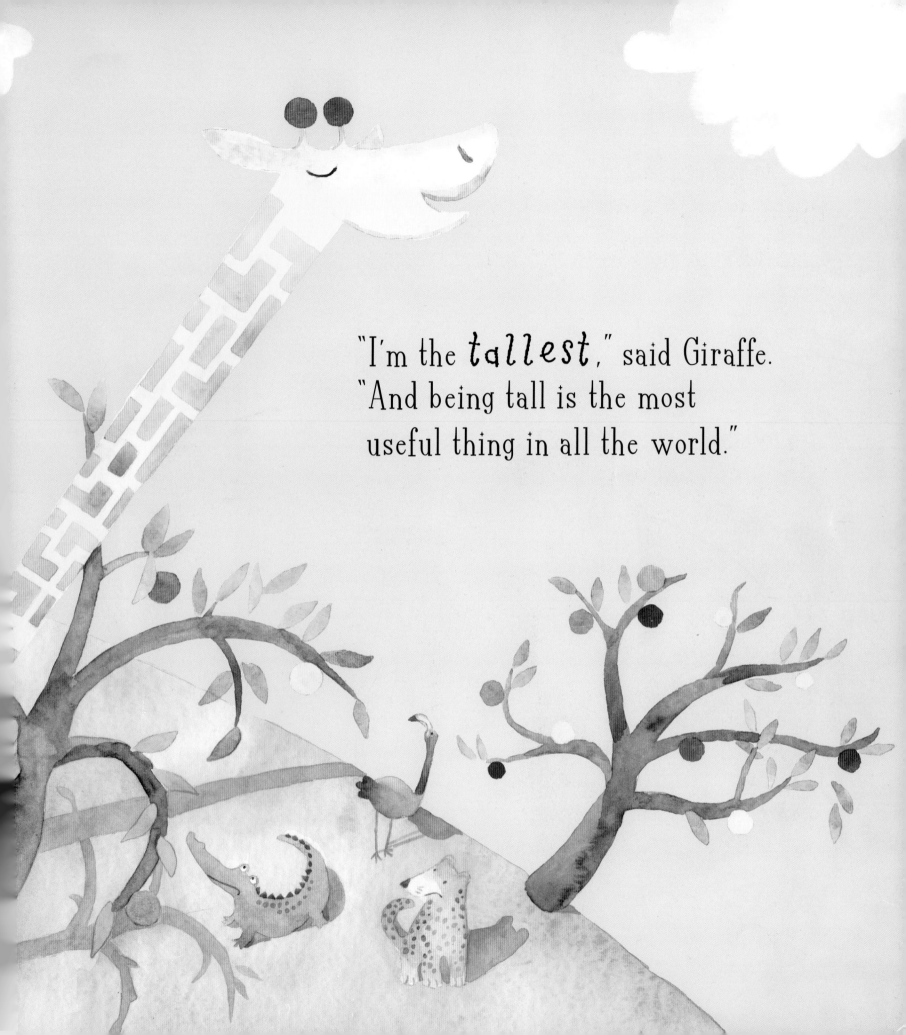

"I'm the **tallest**," said Giraffe.
"And being tall is the most
useful thing in all the world."

The other animals

stretched

as high as they could…

But none of the other animals
could stretch as high as
Giraffe. They didn't like that
Giraffe was the tallest.

Only Raccoon was happy for Giraffe.

"Oh, you are very tall," he said. "You must be a hundred times taller than me. I'm so happy that you are tall."

Raccoon started **jumping**

and **clapping** his hands

and dancing his **happiest** dance.

"Well, I'm the **spikiest**," said Porcupine.
"Spikes keep me safe from danger and make me pretty."

None of the animals were
spiky, and it made them jealous.
Only Raccoon was happy for Porcupine.

"Yes, you are spiky and pretty," said Raccoon.
"No one is as spiky as you are. It makes me
want to dance my **happiest** dance."

"Pretty?!" squealed Pig.
"Pretty means to be
nice and round.
I am the prettiest."

"Color is important, not shape," said Frog.
"I am green, and green is the best color.

The grass is green...

...the trees are green...

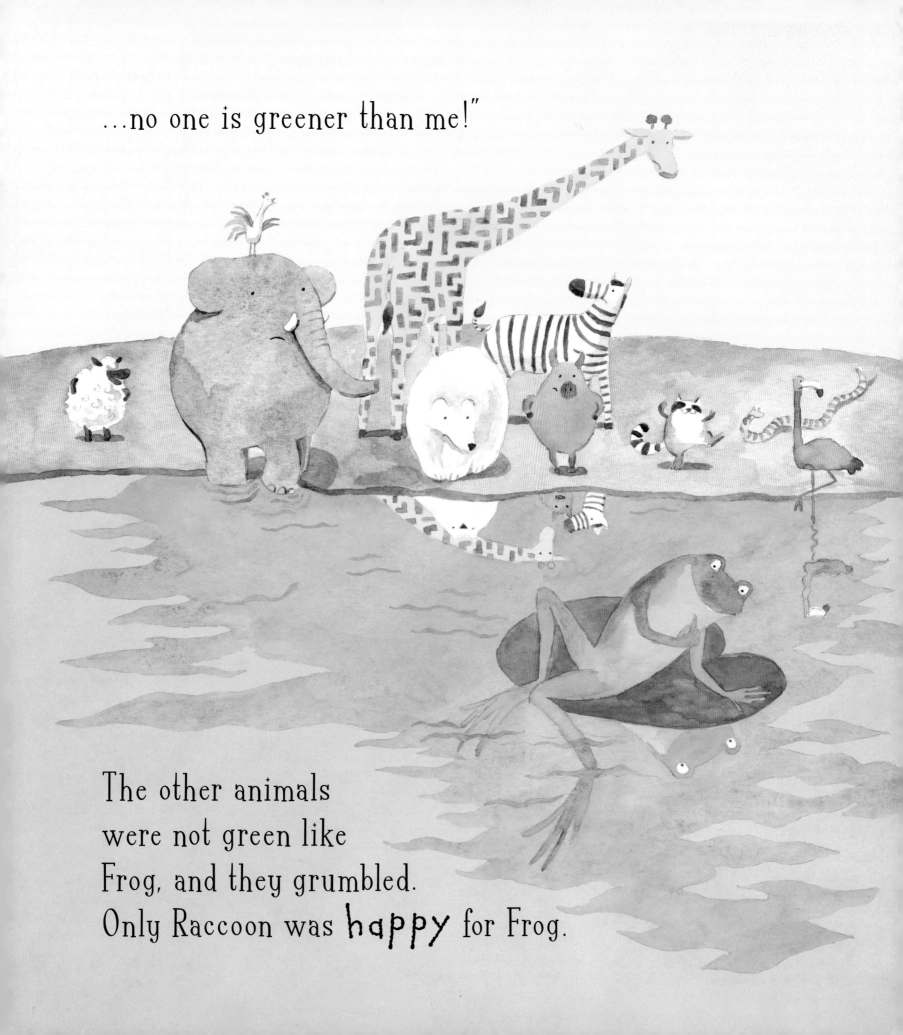

...no one is greener than me!"

The other animals
were not green like
Frog, and they grumbled.
Only Raccoon was **happy** for Frog.

The animals all started to boast that *they* were the best.

"I can jump the **highest**."

"I'm the **stripiest**."

"I'm the most **colorful**."

"I'm the **spottiest**."

"I'm happy that Giraffe is *tall*, Porcupine is *spiky*,
Pig is **round**, and Frog is *green*," said Raccoon.

"You're all so wonderful and different—
it makes me want to dance my **happiest** dance!"

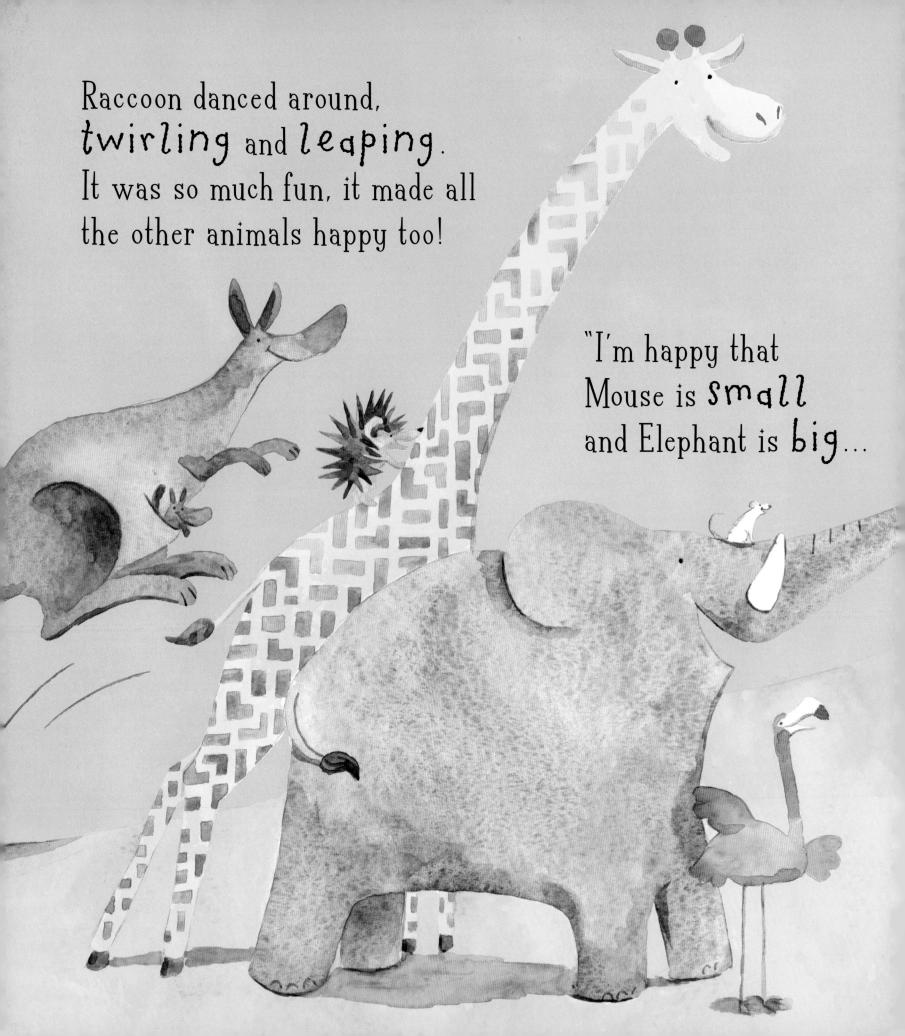

Raccoon danced around, **twirling** and **leaping**. It was so much fun, it made all the other animals happy too!

"I'm happy that Mouse is **small** and Elephant is **big**...

...I'm happy that Snake is *long* and Leopard is *spotty*."

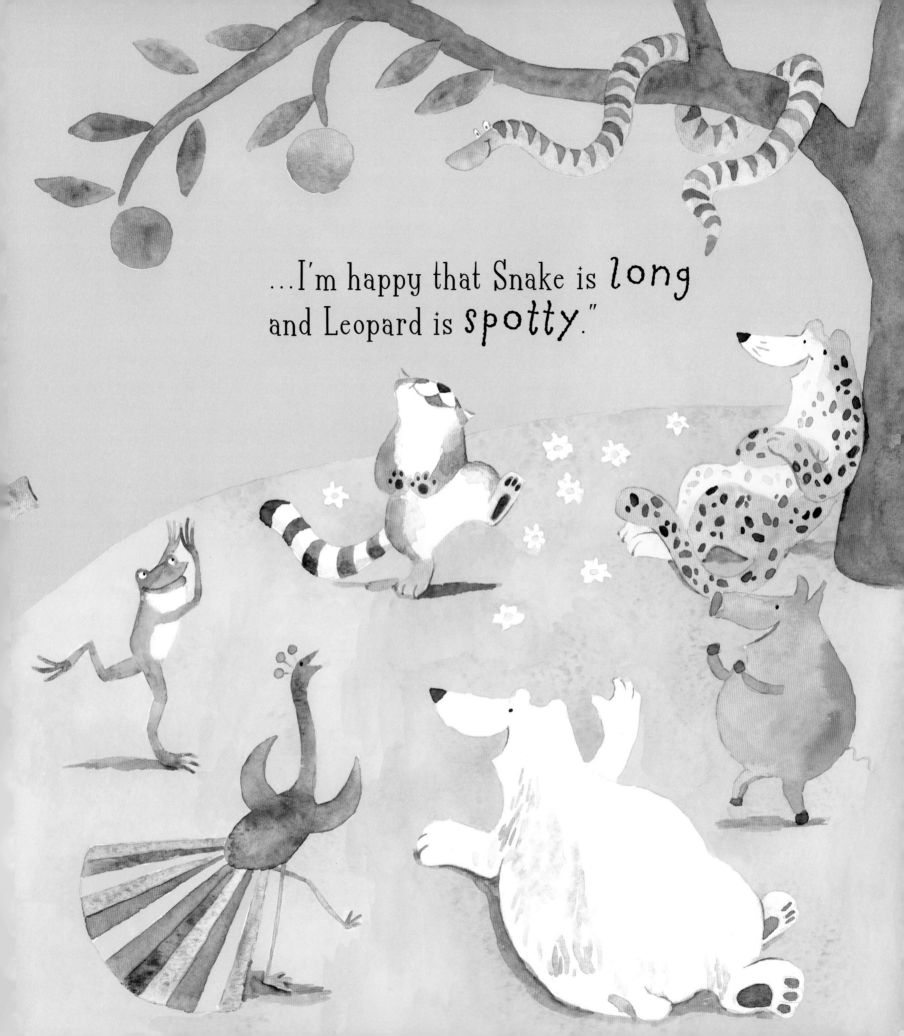

They all danced the happiest dance—
but Raccoon was happiest of all.

"I'M THE HAPPIEST!"

Next steps

Show the children the cover again. Could they have guessed what the story is about from looking at the cover?

This book features lots of different animals from all over the world. Can the children spot an animal from Africa? Can they spot an animal from the Arctic? Ask the children if they have ever been to a zoo. Which animal did they like the most and why? Have they got a favorite animal?

Try playing the following game: Ask the children to think of an animal and use just one word that best describes it. The rest of the group should then guess what the animal is.

Discuss the story with the children. Explain to them that everyone is different but that we're all equally important. Ask the children how they would describe themselves in one word. What feature are they most proud of?

Ask the children if they like hearing about other people's good qualities and achievements. Have they ever been jealous of a friend or family member because they did well at something? Explain to the children that it's important to appreciate other people's qualities.

Ask the children why they think Raccoon is so happy. What makes the children happy?